We hope you enjoy this book.
Please return or renew it by the due date.
You can renew it at **www.norfolk.gov.uk/libraries**
or by using our free library app. Otherwise you can
phone **0344 800 8020** - please have your library
card and pin ready.
You can sign up for email reminders too.

NORFOLK COUNTY COUNCIL
LIBRARY AND INFORMATION SERVICE

First published 2020 by Walker Books Ltd, 87 Vauxhall Walk, London SE11 5HJ. • This edition published 2021 • 10 9 8 7 6 5 4 3 2 1
Text and illustrations © 2020 Daisy Hirst • The right of Daisy Hirst to be identified as the author and illustrator of this work
has been asserted by her in accordance with the Copyright, Designs and Patents Act 1988 • This book has been typeset in
Stempel Schneidler • Printed in China • All rights reserved. No part of this book may be reproduced, transmitted or stored
in an information retrieval system in any form or by any means, graphic, electronic or mechanical, including photocopying,
taping and recording, without prior written permission from the publisher. • British Library Cataloguing in Publication
Data: a catalogue record for this book is available from the British Library • ISBN 978-1-4063-9451-1 • www.walker.co.uk

I Like Trains

Daisy Hirst

WALKER BOOKS

AND SUBSIDIARIES

LONDON · BOSTON · SYDNEY · AUCKLAND

I like playing with my train.

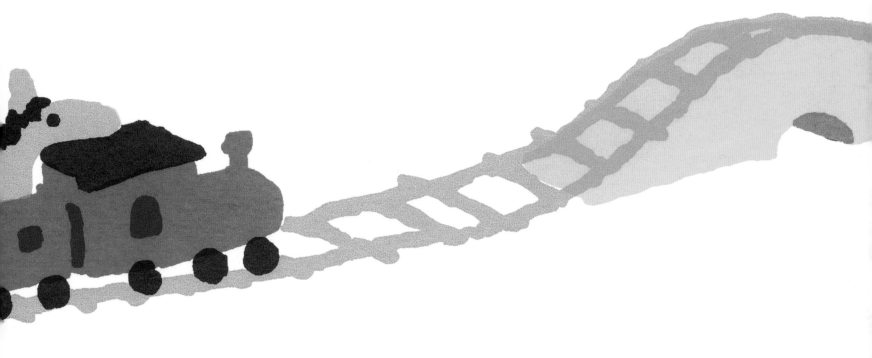

I like putting all the
animals on board so they
can go off on a journey.

Sometimes I drive
a train of my own

and I like reading
books about trains.

long trains

short trains

Louisa

trains
with faces

Bullet Train

Freight

fast trains

slow trains

trains
in races

But the best
thing of all is
when we go to
the station to
catch the train
ourselves.

We buy two
tickets and find
the right platform.

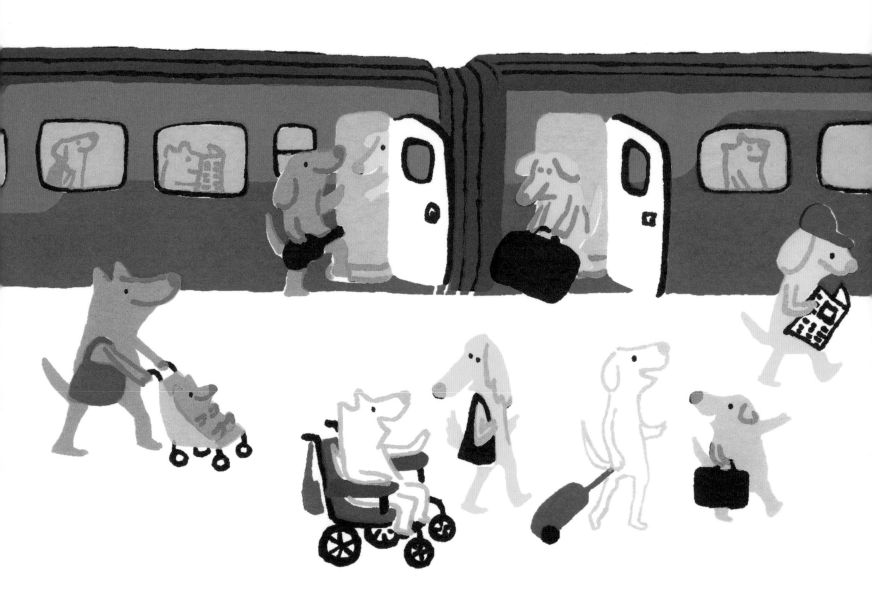

We choose
some seats
by a window and then
the train sets off.

Through the window I see ...

houses and gardens,

trucks and cars,

flats and factories

and boats on a river.

I see fields and trees,

horses and sheep,

darkness in a tunnel

and another train

whooshing by.

The train slows down and

stops and then at last I see ...

Granny!

I tell Granny all
about the journey and
draw her a picture.

Then there's
just time to visit
my favourite
playground!

I love playing
trains with
Granny.